For Penny and Grandpa

Special thanks to Linda, Mom, Judy H., Connie H., Jon Klassen, Steve Turk, LeUyen Pham, Kazu Kibuishi, Chris Appelhans, and Dan Santat

Published by Roaring Brook Press
Roaring Brook Press is a division of Holtzbrinck Publishing Holdings Limited Partnership
120 Broadway, New York, NY 10271
mackids.com

Library of Congress Cataloging-in-Publication Data
Names: Zhu, Ben, 1980– author, illustrator. • Title: Dessert island / Ben Zhu. • Description: First edition. | New York: Roaring Brook Press, 2021. | Audience: Ages 3–6. | Audience: Grades K–1. | Summary: Monkey is stuck on an island made of desserts, and Fox on one made of dirt and rocks, but as time passes, fortunes change and they learn about sharing and caring. • Identifiers: LCCN 2020039929 | ISBN 9781250763303 (hardcover) • Subjects: CYAC: Islands—Fiction. | Monkeys—Fiction. | Foxes—Fiction. | Sharing—Fiction. | Caring—Fiction. | Conservation of natural resources—Fiction. Classification: LCC PZ7.1.Z53 Des 2021 | DDC [E]—dc23 • LC record available at https://lccn.loc.gov/2020039929

Our books may be purchased in bulk for promotional, educational, or business use. Please contact your local bookseller or the Macmillan Corporate and Premium Sales Department at (800) 221-7945 ext. 5442 or by email at MacmillanSpecialMarkets@macmillan.com.

First edition, 2021 • Book design by Aram Kim

The illustrations in this book were created with acrylic and colored pencil on cold press illustration board, with minor modifications and editing in Adobe Photoshop.

Printed in China by Hung Hing Off-set Printing Co. Ltd., Heshan City, Guangdong Province

1 3 5 7 9 10 8 6 4 2

DESSERT ISLAND

Ben Zhu

Roaring Brook Press

New York

I am stuck on a dessert island.
It is made of chocolate, frosting, and berries.

I am stuck on a desert island.
It is made of dirt and rocks.

I am very lucky!

I am very hungry.

Oh no!
I didn't really need that anyway.

Oh boy!
I really needed this.

I can't eat one more bite . . .

I just need one more thing . . .

RAIN?

WATER!

I think my island got smaller.

I think my plant got taller.

I am very worried.

I am very excited.

I can't wait . . .

I can't wait!

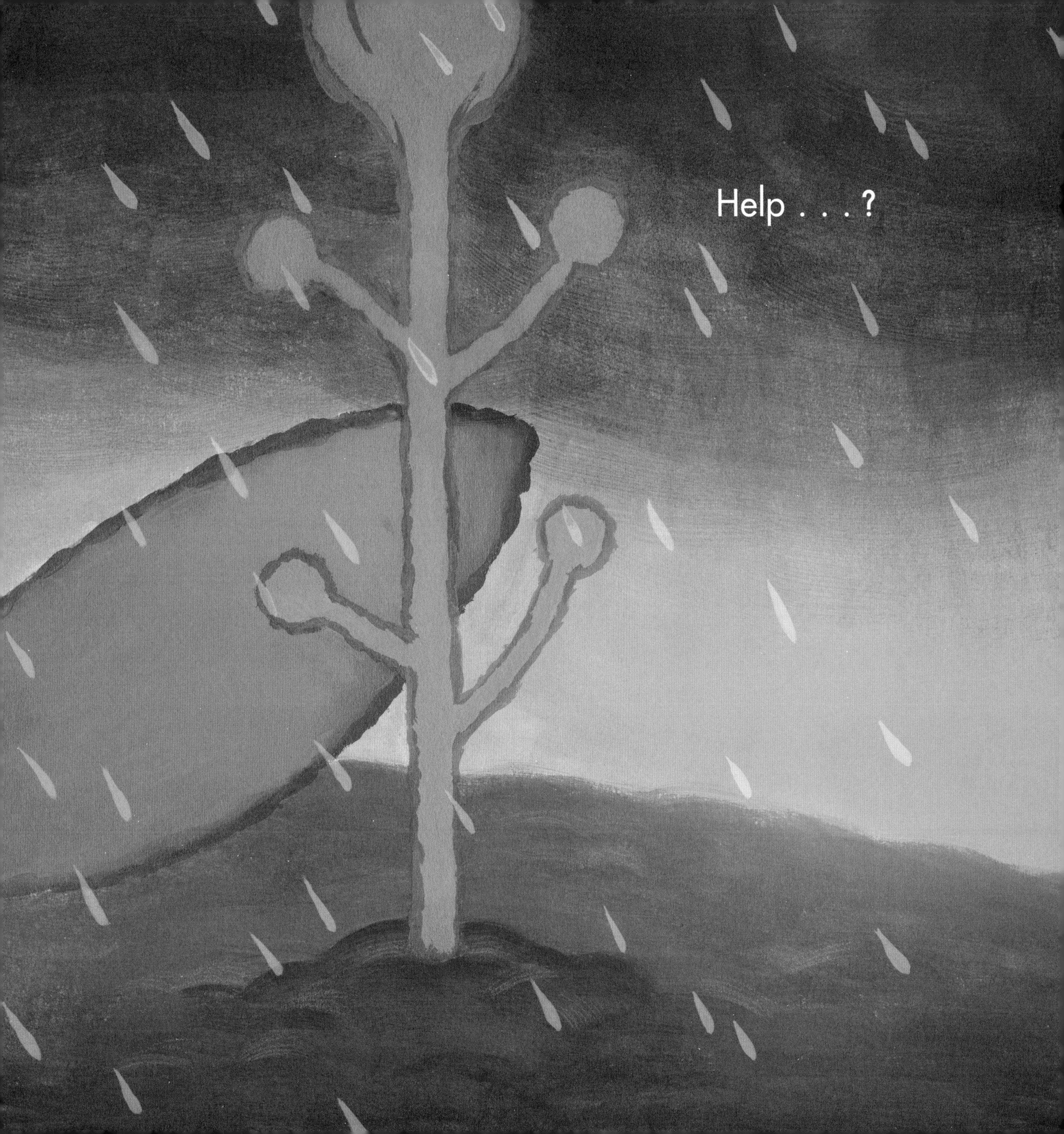

Help . . . ?

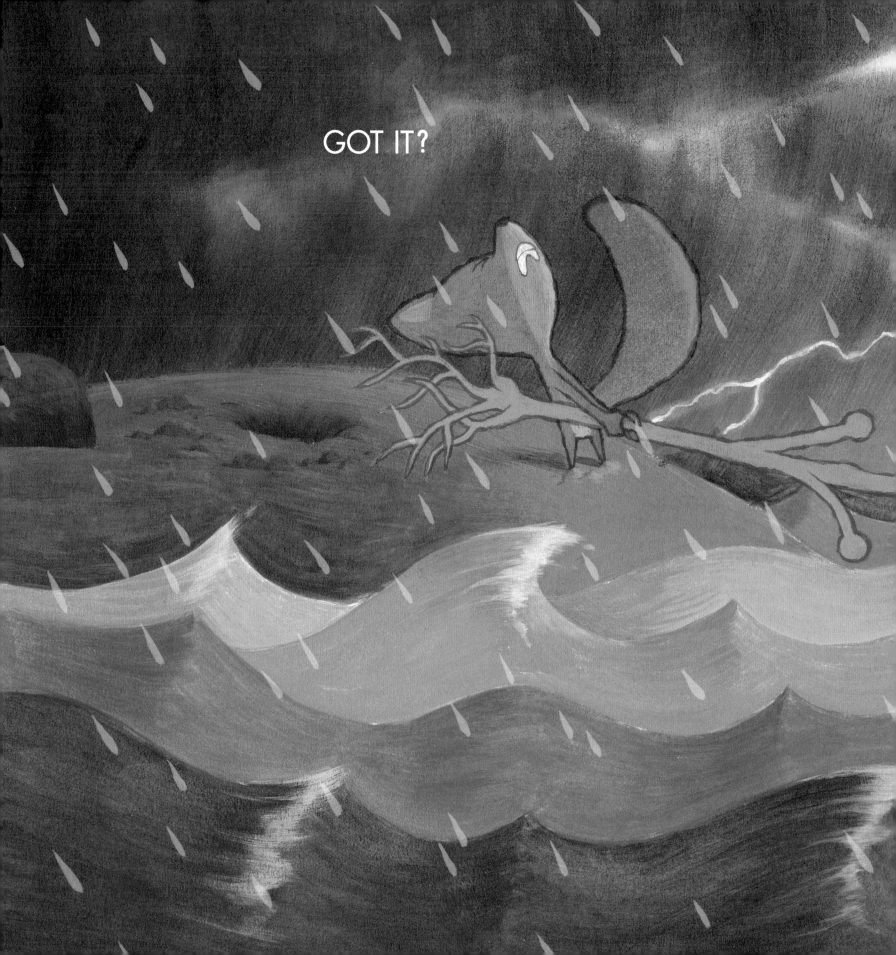

You're welcome.

I am very hungry.

I have . . .

We are on

a desert island.

We are very lucky.